Walt Disney's Bambi

ADAPTED BY LISA ANN MARSOLI

This is the story of the young prince of the forest, Bambi. Read along with me as we embark on an exciting adventure. You will know it is time to turn the page when you hear this sound.... Just follow along, and enjoy this wonderful tale about Bambi and friends.

One spring morning, the creatures of the forest awoke to exciting news.

"The new prince is born!" Thumper the rabbit told them. Everyone gathered in the thicket to see the baby deer and offer their congratulations.

"I think I'll call him Bambi," the proud mother announced. Still tired, Bambi looked at his visitors and went back to sleep.

Soon Bambi was old enough to take his first
wobbly steps.

With his mother following closely behind him,
Bambi explored the forest.

He met lots of animal families—a family of quail and
possums, and a friendly mole, too!

Thumper the rabbit and his family were excited when Bambi
came to visit them. The lively bunnies eagerly introduced Bambi
to birds and butterflies.

They even taught him to say his very first word—"bird"!

One morning, as Bambi sniffed among some blossoms, he discovered a skunk. His new friend cheerfully agreed when Bambi decided to name him Flower.

Bambi, Thumper, and Flower had fun romping together. But when it began to rain, Bambi decided he had had enough adventure for one day!

Soon Bambi was old
enough to accompany his
mother to the meadow. He
couldn't wait to graze and
kick up his heels in the wide
open space.
"You must never rush out
on the meadow!" Bambi's
mother warned him.

She stepped out first, making sure no danger was near. Deciding
it was safe, she signaled Bambi to join her.

In the meadow, Bambi was surprised by a frog jumping in the grass. He playfully chased it back to its pond.

In the water, he saw the reflection of a young doe. Bambi felt so shy he could barely speak.

The deer's name was Faline, and she wasn't shy at all. In fact, she was full of mischief!

Suddenly, a group of stags sprang onto the meadow. Their majestic leader stopped and gazed right at Bambi. The stag was Bambi's father.

"He is the Great Prince of the Forest," Bambi's mother explained.

Moments later, a shot rang out! All of the deer began to flee. Bambi couldn't find his mother, but his father led him to safety, where he was soon reunited with her.

Winter arrived, bringing snow and ice.

Thumper tried to teach Bambi how to slide across the frozen pond. Bambi slid, though not standing up! Whee!

The pair crashed into Flower's den. The little skunk just stretched and went back to sleep. He was getting ready to hibernate through the cold months ahead.

As winter wore on, Bambi and his mother had difficulty find-
ing food growing in the cold forest.

"I'm awful hungry, Mother," Bambi complained.

Finally, they spotted a patch of grass poking through the snow.
But before they could enjoy their meal, Bambi's mother sensed
danger. Man was in the forest.

"Bambi! Quick! The thicket!" she ordered.

"And don't look back!"

Bambi ran as fast as he could as shots rang through the trees. When he stopped, his mother was not behind him.

Bambi's father, the Great Prince of the Forest, appeared through the snow.

"Your mother can't be with you anymore," he said.

The heartbroken fawn followed the stag into the forest. His father would take care of him now.

When spring arrived, Bambi was all grown up. This time when he saw Faline, he wasn't shy. The two became friends, and traveled the woods together.

Then Man came to the forest again. His hunting dogs trapped Faline on a ledge. Bambi bravely fought them off and Faline escaped. But Bambi's life was still in danger.

The hunters came closer, as Bambi weakened from his wounds. Suddenly, the Great Prince appeared.

"You must get up!" he commanded.

Man's campfire had spread, and the flames were coming closer. Bambi struggled, but he managed to follow his father across the river to an island of safety, where Faline was waiting.

One year later, the woods were green and brimming with life once more. Spring had brought with it, not one, but two new additions to the forest family—Faline and Bambi's newborn fawns!

The happy new family settled into the forest, where they lived happily ever after.